MEET
Bacteria!

Rebecca Bielawski

www.booksbeck.com

There is a world so tiny,

You can't see it with just your eyes.

You need to use
a microscope,

To see it
a bigger size.

The tiny fellows that live there are bacteria,

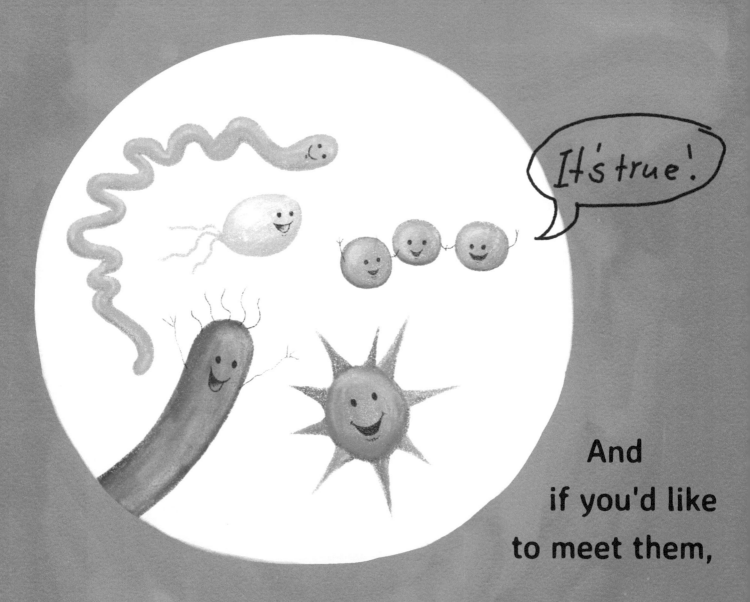

And
if you'd like
to meet them,

They'd like to meet you too.

They're everywhere,
In dirt, in air,
Although they can't be seen,
On walls and doors,
On chairs and floors,
And cracks, there
in between.

"I like frozen places,

I live in snow and ice."

"I live in the water too,
My place is in the sea."

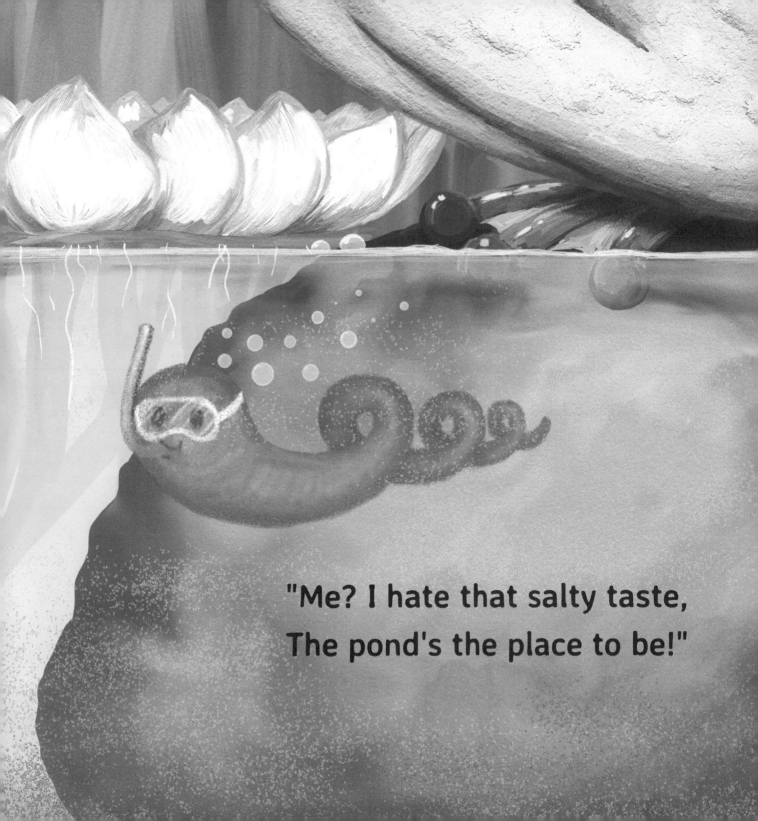

"Me? I hate that salty taste,
The pond's the place to be!"

If they find something that's yummy,
That they'd like to eat for lunch,
They multiply so quickly...

First there's one,

Then there's a bunch!

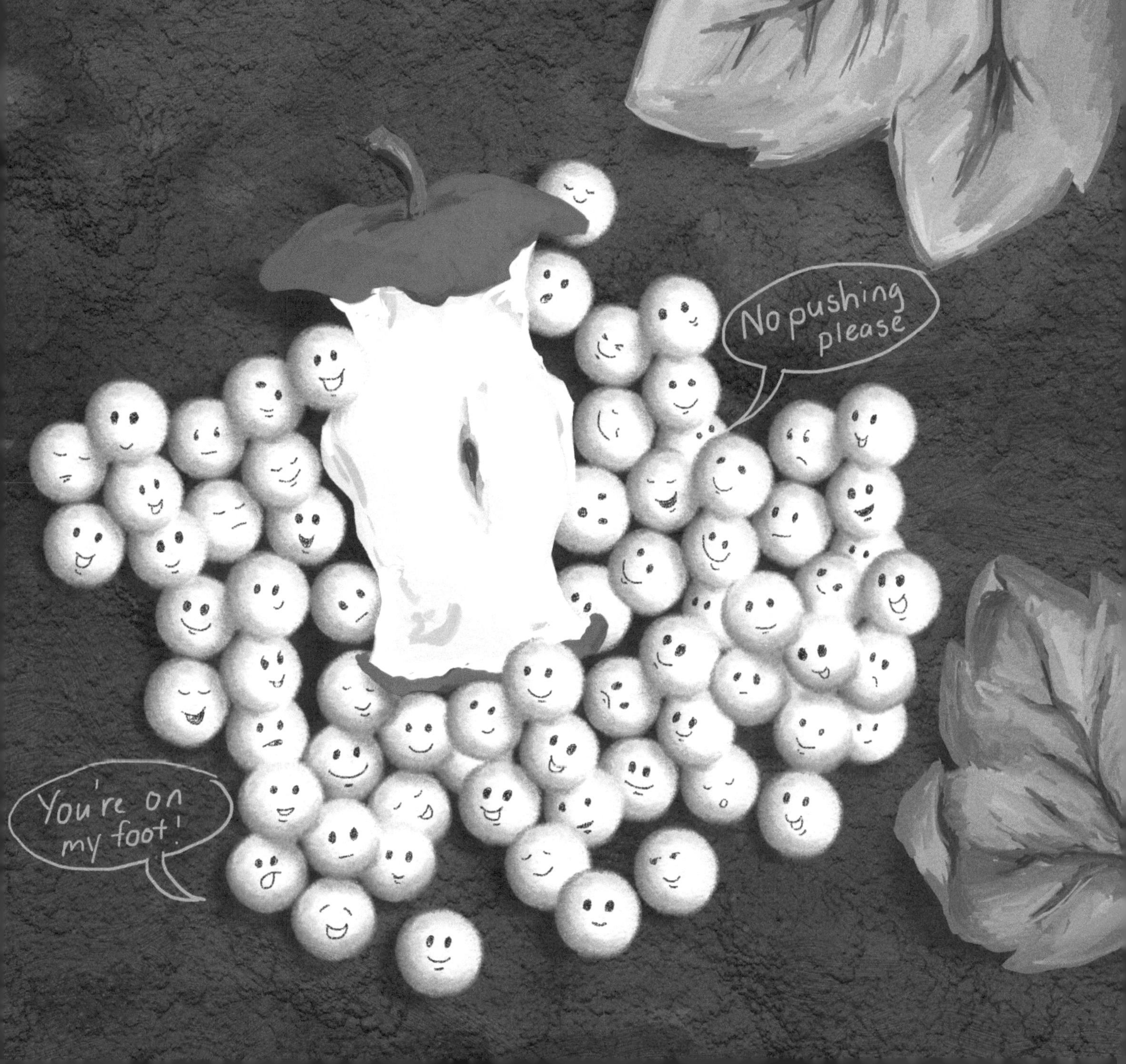

Some of them are naughty,
   To make us sick's their aim.

When you get a belly ache,
Sometimes they're the ones to blame.

da dee dee

dum dee dee

So, after
the toilet,

And before
your food,
I hope,

You don't forget to wash
your hands,
With water and
with soap!

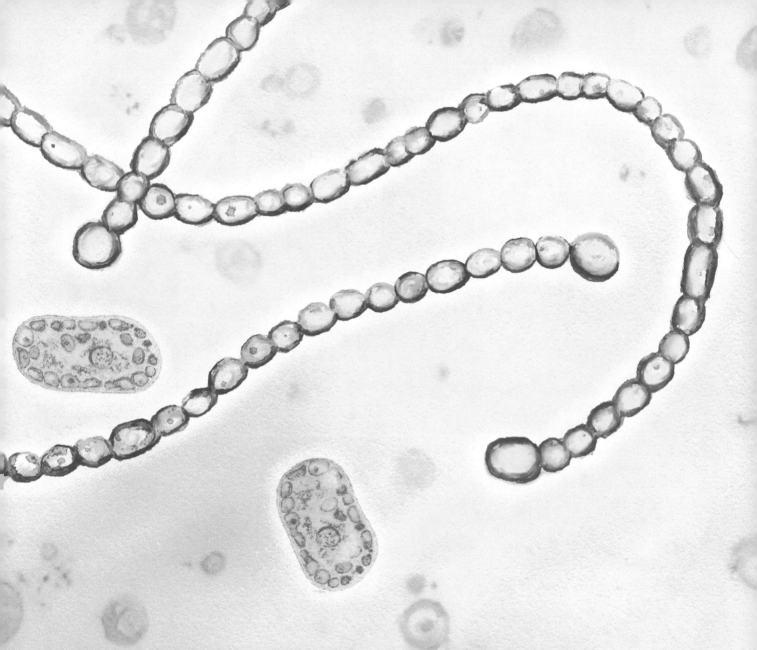

Most of them don't bother us,
They are our little neighbours.

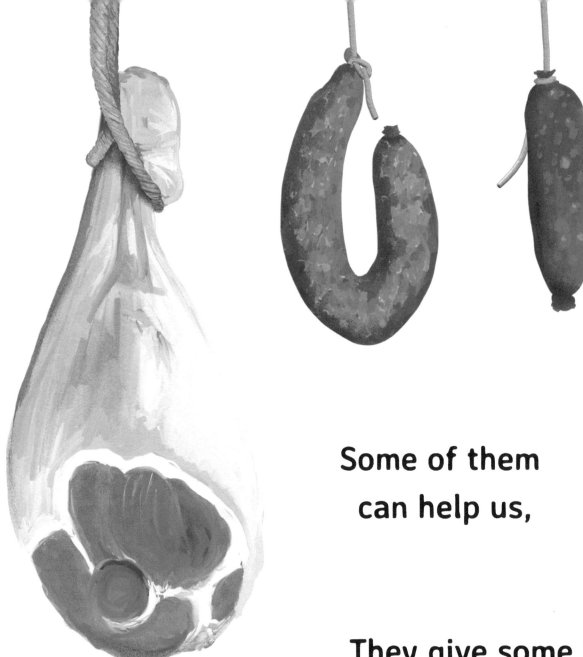

Some of them
can help us,

They give some food
their flavours.

Bacteria make
yogurt,

And stinky cheeses too.

Some help by eating rubbish,
That's a yucky job to do!

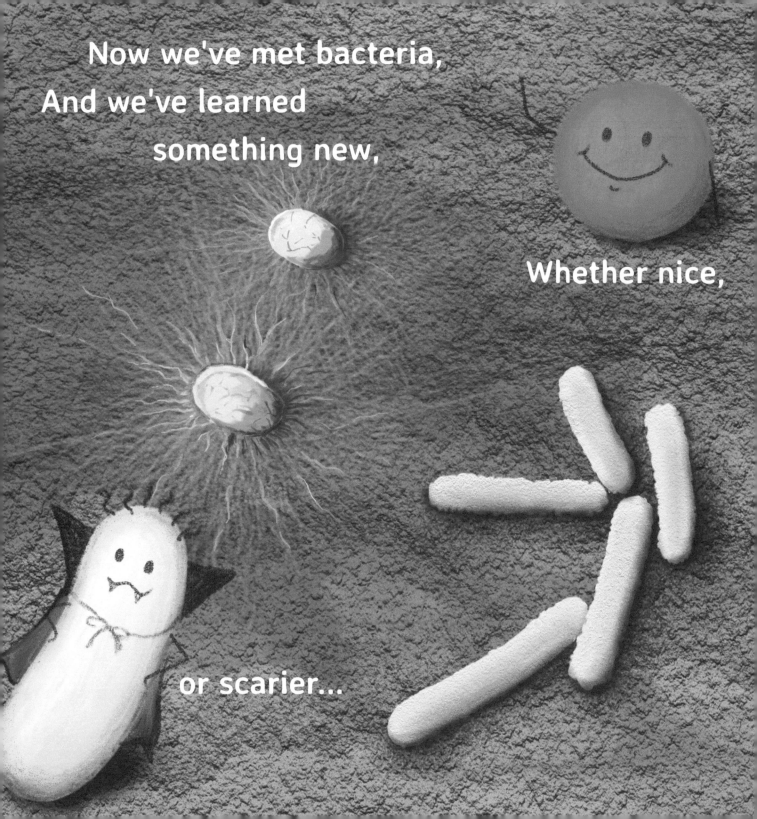

They're part of our world too.

The End

Bacteria Shapes

circle

rod

spiral

bunch

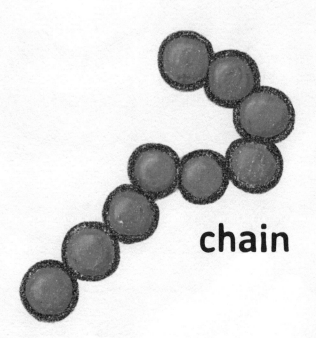

chain

MUMMY NATURE
SERIES

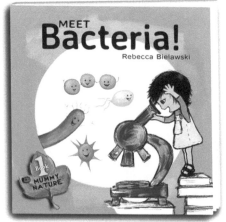

More children's books

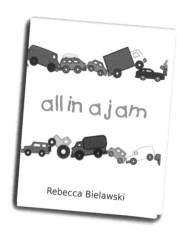

See preview pages, book planning sketches and author articles
and stay up to date on book promos and new releases by Rebecca Bielawski
Ebooks and print books in English and Spanish

www.booksbeck.com

Printed in the USA
CPSIA information can be obtained
at www.ICGtesting.com
LVHW062310010124
767923LV00014B/29

* 9 7 8 8 4 9 4 6 7 1 5 0 0 *